#2

SUMMER 2024

I0646573

MIDSUMMER DREAM HOUSE LITERARY & ARTS MAGAZINE

CALIFORNIA

Midsummer Dream House
San Diego, California
United States

Cover Photography
by Ashley Kaplan

Paperback ISBN: 979-8-9917450-8-6
Print ISSN: 3064-7819
Printed in the United States

midsummer dream house

Editor-in-Chief
Emma Grey Rose

Editor
George du Bois

CONTENTS

POETRY
JEFFREY ZABLE
The Lesson, Seemingly in Complete Agreement / 1
SHAUN ANTHONY MCMICHAEL
Boy, Shark / 2
SUT PHAL
Free-Form Haikus 5-7-5 / 3
STARRY KRUEGER
Big / 4
PAUL HOSTOVSKY
What happened with you guys anyway? / 5
Cocksure / 7
NICHOLAS GROOMS
Mourning, Mid Afternoon / 8
JOHN GREY
Relative Happiness / 9
BRANDON INGALLS
Night Moves / 11
JC REILLY
Heart-bird / 13
MARCOS ORO
Sun / 14

MEMOIRS
JERRY CHIEMEKE
Fantasising About You Being Someone Who Loves Me / 15
JONATHAN WOO
Ariana / 18

FICTION
GARTH WOLKOFF
Less Important / 20
HUINA ZHENG
Rainy Day / 25

CRYSTAL W. PILLIFANT
Maggie and Frank / 26
KEVIN MANDEL
Our Grateful Dead Story / 28

ART
EDWARD MICHAEL SUPRANOWICZ
***Bad Vibes* / i**
Digital Painting
ASHLEY KAPLAN
***Body* / iv**
Photography
PIA QUINTANO
***Doorstep, Green Peace* / 46**
Acrylic on Canvas

BIOGRAPHIES / 42

JEFFREY ZABLE

THE LESSON

Years ago when I was a student at City College
of San Francisco I had this photography teacher
who confessed to me that he was married for three weeks:

"We met at a party. Both of us were drunk. Went home
together that night and the next day decided to go to Las Vegas
and get married. Things went fairly well the first week.
Less so the second week. And by the third week we were
at each other's throats. It's lucky one of us didn't kill the other!"

"What did you learn from the experience?" I asked him and he replied,
"Don't drink and get married! That's mainly what I learned."

SEEMINGLY IN COMPLETE AGREEMENT

Accidentally giving the woman an extra twenty
for my groceries at the checkout counter, she hands
it back and says, "You obviously didn't mean to give me
this extra 20!"

"Wow! an honest woman!" I respond. "You must have
serious problems getting by in a world like this. I guess
you'll just have to carry on as best you can!"

Smiling at what I said, she replies, "You got it!
That's always been my problem. . . staying on the straight
and narrow. I guess it's too late to change now!"

Smiling back, I answer, "I certainly understand!
I've always stayed on the straight and narrow as well.
Hopefully, we'll both be rewarded in the afterlife!"

To which she nods, seemingly in complete agreement.

SHAUN ANTHONY MCMICHAEL

BOY, SHARK

You hurt women. It's what happens. The man thinks
back to when he was a boy. Women filled that living room,
his mother off somewhere at work or in the kitchen.
Cousin, Auntie, Grandma. They watched him play,
amused especially by his shark-toy-phase.
Shark boy! Hey sharkie, one of the women teased
the man-to-be. *I'm not a shark! I'm a boy.*
he blabbed until a wily one grabbed him. *The shark started
small and cute too. Like everything! How
do you know you won't turn into a great white?*

The boy went silent as if from the ocean's depths
in narrowing upward spirals he circled
until he was just below the fishy-looking feet
of the women who were not his mother.
Their screams confirmed the fear he sensed
had taken his mother's place. He wanted
to make the fear go away and thought he could
by coming closer and swallowing the fear whole.
The women screamed louder and kicked. Their flesh
caught on his canines. Through the inky red clouds,
he couldn't see but felt the pieces of fear
drift down to where he idled, waiting to wake up,
the fear keeping him from opening his eyes.

How could this have happened? he thinks every time
after hurting a woman, as a boy opening his eyes
to the nightmare truth. It's happened. He's turned
into a great white
of a man.

FREE-FORM HAIKUS 5-7-5

"Muted sound no noise
entering a throwback scene
you visit my dreams"

"Nights that reminisce
sun rising the morning bliss
days of missing you"

"Pleasurable pain
photographic memories
letters with no name"

"Casting ink dream scene
shaded art classical page
papers no faces"

STARRY KRUEGER

BIG

I am doing things, Big Sister.
Money things.
Legal things.
Golden California things.

I put your money in the bank.
And I read your name on lots of pages.
With the word, "deceased" on every
line.

Like I forgot.

I wonder about your pain.
That you kicked through doors
And poured out of cereal bowls
And couldn't find a bottle
Big enough to drown.

Is that why you set records
For walking on your hands?
Did the world make more sense
When you turned it upside down?

I wish I could go back to the grown ups
And teach them how to spell trauma
And give them extra mittens
To keep your small hands warm

And make the world safe for your wild
And believe the words you said

And tell them you do not have to
choose
Between being in pain and being

"smart"

You taught me things, Big Sister.
The electric slide.
People lie.
Don't eat the whole artichoke.
Heal or die.

PAUL HOSTOVSKY

WHAT HAPPENED WITH YOU GUYS ANYWAY?

because what I heard was
you both walked away
from your unhappy marriages
two children each
to be with each other
that it started at work
the way it sometimes does
that you'd worked together
closely the kind of closely
that can sometimes lead to play
the kind of play that can
turn serious in a heartbeat
a head-tilt a glance then a glancing away
then a looking back again
a smile that turns suddenly hungry
which I heard it did
and it turned everyone against you
when they heard what you did
leaving your families for each other
but I want you to know
when I heard I was first of all
happy for you and maybe a little
titillated to think of you both
finding love among the cubicles
right there on the desk or maybe
under it on the floor
and when I heard the grumblings
and judgments and condemnations
I felt compelled to send you
that Hallmark card did you get it?
because *Congratulations*
seemed the right thing to say somehow
but then more recently I heard
that you're not together anymore

WHAT HAPPENED WITH YOU GUYS ANYWAY?

or rather you're still working together
but you're not *together* together
and I thought to myself that's gotta be hard
and I know it's none of my business but
what happened with you guys anyway?

COCKSURE

I haven't been sure of my cock since that day
it refused to stand up when it was supposed to–
which was the day we were scheduled to "do it"
one truant spring afternoon in my father's house
when I was 16 and Faith was 18 and naked
and cocksure and straddling me on the bed, whispering
"fuck me, fuck me." I'm not exactly sure why
it wouldn't stand up. It may have had something to do
with the age differential, or the vertical differential,
or the breathy imperative coming down from on high,
or the several weightinesses: There was the weightiness
of Faith herself, who wasn't twiggy, chafing and bobbing
on top of me; and the weightiness of the prospect
of losing my virginity; and the weightiness of her position
as the editor of the literary magazine vis a vis my position
as the diffident young poet whose exquisite death poem
had blown her and the entire literary magazine staff away
with its lively metaphors and imagery and weightiness,
which I borrowed from the weightiness of the dying
of my father, from colon cancer, only two months before.
It was his poem and it was his death. And the bed was
his bed–he had moved out of my parents' bedroom
when the pain got so bad he had to be alone–on which
Faith was alternately declaiming lines from my poem
and breathlessly adding the refrain "fuck me, fuck me"
while I lay beneath her, cock soft, in my father's
sickbed, dying to fuck her, unable to, wanting to die.

First published in *Beaver Magazine,* 2021

NICHOLAS GROOMS

MOURNING, MID AFTERNOON

There is nothing like self-tyranny in the morning,
A heart and mind that cannot peacefully coexist
an accidental splash of the kettle water's scald
the inescapable smell of wet dog
squish to peel are the last two bananas, ripe
chiquita brown skin ripened darker than mine
tumble dry piles of linens to fold
mean mugging the baby socks I need to match
little shirts   little pants   little food stains
the color of varicose veins
afternoon cat naps, declawed
by the words in an overheard song
tears rolling out like party streamers
decorating my fleshy cheeks
And to the tune of the Beatles hit,
I imagine writing out *"HELP"*
across the front lawn
in letters made out of Hefty bags
and household appliances
piles of dirty dishes
stained couch cushions
soiled wet diapers of leaking angst
hoping an overhead plane will see
my smoke signal tokes of longed escape
as my sanity begins to careen,
swallowed by the incorrect thoughts
I continue to perceive

JOHN GREY

RELATIVE HAPPINESS

Don't come to me with your relative happiness.
Don't tell me how
pain is not quite so bad these days,
that the half empty cup you've been toting around
from poetry reading in the Bronx
to late night tears in my apartment
is now half full.
Don't share with me how your neuroses
are now just character strains,
those suicidal impulses merely
an incentive to slit the veins
of one part of a life
so the rest of it can go free.

I don't want to know that
with nothing more than
a third floor flat and a second hand television
and a jug of wine and maybe
two or three close friends,
you zapped up all of those heart wounds,
manufactured the platonic lover
you always longed for
out of dust mites and spiderwebs.
Your family are dead.
Well here's a new family
made of cheese and crackers,
good books, the telephone.

I don't want to be around
when you say that if you get over a cold
then you've gotten over a cancer.
I want everything to matter so much
that nothing else matters.
I want to carry my hurt to the grave,

RELATIVE HAPPINESS

never recover from anything that ails me.
I don't want a picture of reality
that you can stick on a wall
like a framed view of the steady, reliable ocean.
I need it to grow its tumors in me,
so big, so toxic, they make themselves
known to every feeling, every thought.

If I get up from this and admit to myself
that I can get over it,
then it never really happened.

Nothing has happened.
I want my plagues to devour me,
not strengthen me,
my bankruptcies to leave me penniless,
my broken love affairs to
really break beyond repair.

So keep your new dignity, new pride,
new ways of dealing with the world
to yourself.
Relative happiness is a fraud.
It never was and never could be
the happiness we deserve.

BRANDON INGALLS

NIGHT MOVES

He talks too much, can't help himself.
It is always dark here. Sometimes

  you wave your hand before your face
  just to see the air stir.

Graham came by way of South Carolina.
He claims his father is a sheriff

  operating out of Kolb County, a good man
  but not the type to be trifled with. Both hands

knuckled like they're brass, a high pitch
clicking in the tall weeds. June

  she doesn't talk much. Says her prayers quiet.
  In the night, the air's a heavy fold

and dew its own form of smother. Our mama left
in May, before the air was a stifling thistle,

  the fields crackling with their heat. So we left
  with a compass. Leathered straps. Saltines. Two

hollow-bored tubes to pitch the tent, and my brother
won't quit crying about the insects

  and the horseflies buzzing 'round his neck.
  We keep our eyes on the flame,

those orange tongues licking at our palms.
My brother crying, and Graham's talking

  an endless chatter

NIGHT MOVES

whispering out the holler, snaking down the trailhead

to a shore that won't quit.

Winner of the Summer 2024
Midsummer Dream House Poetry Contest

JC REILLY

HEART-BIRD

after Charles Bukowski

There's a bird where my heart should be
wee feathery thing, sparrow plain and small,
I urge it to sing, but rarely to me,

my ears too old to hear tunes clearly.
Others, heartless, come, and recognize its call.
(There's a bird where their hearts should be

too.) All of us stand beneath the orange tree,
our heart-birds holding us each in thrall.
I urge mine to sing, if it must, to me,

and so it does, keeping time, keeping key
with others of its race. Notes rise and fall.
There's a bird where my heart should be;

it knows far too much to be set free,
but it's adapted to my ways, habitual
now. I urge it to sing, if it wants, to me.

I wonder do others take time to see
What their heart-birds get up to at all?
Oh, sweet bird where my heart should be:
Sing, sing, to your heart's content—and to me.

Nominee of the Summer 2024
Midsummer Dream House Poetry Contest

SUN

i.
i cannot hide the bloody mirrored cracked crystal glass
memory of frozen blackened
eyes from birth, anymore, for anyone, I just was born a funny way
pop pop pop
caught in

precisely the quantum flux erased
all notions of place, but not now nor ever the conception of breath,
nor of unearthed, unexpected accompaniment

of invisible oxygen in with a blossoming thought descending into long ocean depths the
deeper the darker the waters came down surrounding everything...

ii.
as well as blood on metal melting right through onto a very large rusted anchor
underwater bearing floating lime-green plants,

slowly underneath aquatic undulations murmuring; waves roaring abruptly
onto the cool absorption of frothing speckled sand the waters reverse back onto themselves

the sun is bright and hot, everywhere touching down with potent splinters cut from
molten jeweled rays

the ocean breadth floats intently above deep sleepy blurry sunken treasures,
steaming mists exhale loudly and evaporate in silence

iii.
a seething primordial sight, bathed
by our ancient sun's canopy of fire
freshly suspended by threads, or webs; and pondering night
...yet seemingly goes away for a while—

JERRY CHIEMEKE

FANTASISING ABOUT YOU BEING SOMEONE WHO LOVES ME

(after JP Saxe)

I don't want to read about the new man that you're loving.

I don't want to see those bright flowers, I don't want to know how he got you a necklace & asked that you turn around so he fits it for you. I once ran my fingers through that hair, I once felt the pulse of that heart, I once drew out hymns from behind those lips.

I don't want to stumble on tweets of how he "makes you feel seen", because it makes me wonder if those Tuesday morning CityTaxi rides from Abraham Adesanya Estate to Falomo, where stolen kisses distracted you from the crushing gridlock, meant nothing to you. I don't want to bump into an Instagram story where you gush about how it's "refreshing to spend the Christmas holiday with someone you like", because it makes me ask myself if Boxing Day of 2020, and the three days that followed, never existed.

The Bible talks about how Love is not jealous, but maybe St. Paul had no idea what he was saying, maybe Jealousy is a feeling stronger than love. Visual images of you straddling someone else unfold like a nightmare to me, and late evening dreams of you curling as you call out the name of another while water gushes from behind your walls, make me sink my teeth into my nails.

Wasn't it almost rhythmic, the way you'd walk in, drop your bag on my couch, head to the kitchen sink to wash your hands, then use the baby wipes and fling them into the bin? I loved watching you take off your top and strut to the bed in lingerie. There was a ring to the way you did it; you seemed so comfortable and knew that the bra would go off before long, but you put it on anyway. You loved Process.

A whiff of your hair was all I needed to send all the blood rushing down there.

There was an earnestness to the way you slowly tucked me inside. In a way,

FANTASISING ABOUT YOU BEING SOMEONE WHO LOVES ME

it showed how much you wanted it, how much you wanted me. There was a melody to the way you breathed out when holding my refrigerator, or my reading table. I meant every letter when I said I didn't want to ever think about you being like that with someone else.

Sometimes the best adventures begin with crippling anxiety, with intense cravings for company occasioned by vulnerability, with convenient arrangements fuelled by post-genocidal paranoia. But sometimes they also begin with a private reading session, with half-decent jollof pasta, with whispers of "hey, can I touch you?" on a mosquito-laden Monday evening by 11.43 pm. Did your sister ever ask about that air conditioner condenser we broke while we...?

You loved to remind me of how annoying I was. For a thing that never had labels, you got a pretty lovely package, especially when you consider the AITA stories that go viral on Reddit.

"I love your touch a little too much...it's easy with you."

Well, why haven't you texted me for nearly five months then? Why are you posting photos of cake deliveries to your office? Why do you keep quoting videos of lovey-dovey couples with approving emojis, just to show everyone that you are now experiencing something similar?

"I want to fight back saying 'I love you' after you've eaten me out so good..."

Maybe we adored each other a lot more than we cared to admit, maybe my insistence on our genetic incompatibility was my own way of displaying cowardice, or maybe your rant about preferring someone from your denomination was a lie you told yourself to deflect from your fear of commitment.

"I get embarrassed whenever my body responds so wantonly to your..."

You're right about the way your body spoke to me, Miss Moneypenny. You loved to tell me about how much of an asshole your boss was, and how he had you work way beyond your job description. I would tease you about it, and the nickname from James Bond's sassy secretary was something you would get used to.

I don't want to see your WhatsApp status updates waxing lyrical about how "being with your soulmate feels different." I melted whenever you touched the nape of my neck, and I had fevers during the weeks we wouldn't talk because we had fought over my attitude of not replying to texts.

"You are tender with me..."

What other words could I have used to describe Love if I wouldn't admit what it was? How long was I going to refrain from conceding that my soul burned for you? But that's the thing with time, I guess. You're not sure of which moment to cherish, until memories are all you're left with.

"What can you do with what you are feeling?"

Moneypenny, maybe tell me that I can have the fact you love(d) me to hold on to, maybe tell me there's still a crack in the door.

A thousand "I-yearn-for-you"s will not open a portal for teleportation. Writing "I miss you" in all the lines of a notebook will not remedy what was unsaid...but what is love, if not sustained regret? Isn't it easier to pine from oceans away? Despair is convenience.

I crave for you in ways that would have priests instructing me to do extended penance at confessionals. I will probably never reach out again, but just let me know this: is your debit card pin still drawn from your birthday?

ARIANA

Maybe it was that she was pretty or that she was really nice to me, or that she always let me play all her video games.

I can remember little moments, like when she was really excited one day that I was going over to her house. Or the time she cried because I had to go home early.

There was the time we went to the elementary fall fair together. She'd given me a couple of extra quarters from her allowance. On the ride home, we were tired and filled with chocolate.

I can't tell you why I told her that I liked her. What does an eight-year-old know about love? But I did it anyway.

It happened on the bus after school. I sat on the bench behind Ariana, alone.

"Why are you sitting back there?" she asked.

"I dunno."

I remember how hot it was inside the bus, but the faux leather seats were almost always cold. I rested my head on the back part of Ariana's seat and looked out the window. The bus was nearly empty, which made it all the more quiet. I had to be careful.

Then it happened all at once.

"I like you," I said.

There, it was out. Silence.

I decided she hadn't heard me, so I opened my mouth to say it again. "I already have a boyfriend," she said.

Eventually we made it back to our stop. I ran to the front of the bus before it had even come to a stop. I heard Ariana call out my name.

I ran. Then, inside the house, I cried. I bawled.

My mother came out from her room to ask me what was wrong. She held me as I tried to explain.

That evening, I plunked down in my room, watching TV for hours. After that I went to the garage, where I played with my Nintendo 64.

I was back in my room when the doorbell rang. I heard my mother open the door. After some chatter, she called up to me.

"Jonathan, there's someone here who wants to see you," she said.

When I came down, Ariana's mother was standing at the door. Ariana stood next to her, hiding in her shadow.

"Jonathan, Ariana wants to speak with you about something," Ariana's mom said. Then she turned and walked
back to her idling van.

Ariana looked at me for a moment, a pained look on her face.

"I'm sorry I lied to you," she said. She looked down at her shoes.

The night air was silent and cool. A chill passed between us. I can't remember what I said to her. Ariana took out a little yellow plush dragon from her jacket and held it out to me. I looked at her, then I took it, and she ran back into her mother's van.

For a week I tried my hardest, but elementary school love is a fickle thing. As with most things over time, the dragon got lost.

GARTH WOLKOFF

LESS IMPORTANT

Why they had our kids come for a seven am class I never knew—so few actually showed up. But I enjoyed the early start time. I taught the 5th- to 7th-grade reading level, which I considered the sweet spot at Frederick Douglass. Students had the vocabulary to write some, read some more, but the high school equivalency exam remained a few years off—we focused on the literacy skills in this class; we focused on the issues at hand.

During the first five days of school that year, two students showed up everyday, Keisha and Anora, two Trinidadian sisters, 18 and 20. They were joined by Sharon and Irie, unrelated but both had stopped going to school in Jamaica at about the same middle-school age and both were now 18. I drank my coffee, had a cheap little CD player to play some very mellow jazz, and read the Times until I could hear the kids walking up the four flights of stairs. The classrooms themselves couldn't have been more beautiful, double-paned and floor-to-ceiling windows overlooking lower Manhattan, downtown Brooklyn, even bits of New York Harbor. With the early light coming in, I'd feel optimistic about the day, my students, my life, my writing, even my romantic prospects. Life is usually better in the morning.

When the girls came in, I shoved my paper in my ragged briefcase and got out the journals and pens I had bought with the small chunk of change the city gave teachers to buy supplies. First thing, the five of us wrote, or, on that morning, Ceejay and Mohamed, also from Trinidad, had shown up, seven of us worked busily, quietly, with Miles Davis playing in the background. Everyday, we'd start writing on one of three topics which I posted on the chalkboard—give students choices, I had learned in graduate school, so I gave choices—and when they couldn't think of anything else to write, they could change to another of the topics or simply empty out what occupied their minds. Write about anything. Just write.

On that Tuesday, though, all six kids came on time, which made me proud of them, as I knew that early morning arrivals taxed them something fierce. Because the students had immigrated to the United States, I chose immigration as the topic. The previous week, we started with five minutes of writing. The day before, Monday, I had upped the time to 10 minutes.

1. Who in your family chose to immigrate to the United States and why?

Did you agree with the person who decided to immigrate?
2. Which do you like better, your home country or where you live now? Why?
3. What kinds of things do immigrants have in common? What are some differences between immigrants?

I went over some of the vocabulary I wanted them to try to use, *immigrant, immigration, homeland, home country, grandmother, grandfather, aunt, uncle, cousin, environment, neighborhood.* By that morning, during journal writing, they could use profanity and didn't need to worry about grammar.

We sat in a circle writing–in grad school, they told us to read when the students read, and write when the students wrote. So that's what I did. There may have been a prohibition against serving coffee to high school students, but in the first years of the new millennium, no one at the Frederick Douglass Literacy Program seemed to follow many of the New York City Education Department's rules–a benign neglect under which Frederick Douglass and it's 200 overaged and under-skilled students toiled in order to pass the high school equivalency exam, except for the few that would also go on to college. So I brought in a coffee maker and some of the kids poured their own every morning, stirred in the non-dairy creamer, added spoon loads of sugar, and fastidiously cleaned up after themselves.

I had taken one class getting my teaching degree that addressed adolescent literacy–I had only taught for two years previously before that day. And in that class I took in grad school, the professor and one of the books we read stressed the importance of ritual. Get your students practicing language every day: writing, reading, speaking, and listening. Seemed right. So after they wrote, we went around the circle and read. Everyday. I thought that would be a tough ask, but after the first day of school a week before, the kids–who were barely younger than me–complied.

Irie means good and friendly, he said on the first day, when we wrote about our names, although that was all he wrote. The next day, he wrote that he was also half Jamaican, which is why his father named him Irie. He impressed me. We had been in school for only five days that year, and his writing got longer everyday. Irie liked to read his writing out loud; today, he wanted to go first.

"Some immigrants are punk-ass bitches."

Although they could write about whatever they felt, the red in his eyes and furrow in his brow surprised me. He didn't look at me, but he looked at each one of the other students. I had been sailing along writing my own response to the immigration prompt, happy that I had six whole students so early in the morning, drinking my coffee.

Ceejay, however, matched the mood that Irie brought in. "Who you calling a bitch?"

I hadn't thought Irie had targeted one group of people. Rather, I thought Irie liked to provoke. He did like to provoke, but this time, he had an agenda.

"You. You and the other rassclaat Trinis."

And just like that, at seven thirty five in the morning, all that beautiful sunlight and optimism that had filled the classroom—new starts, new beginnings—had lost its sheen and became gray.

Both boys stood up. Mohamed stood up. Sharon stood up. Keisha and Anora looked at each other and crossed their arms.

"Hey, hey." Now I stood up. "Come on, let's sit down." I could feel the sweat start in my pits and on my head. No one sat, including me; Keisha and Anora stood up also, although they moved very close to one another.

"Irie. Let's walk back that statement a little. It seems hostile and angry." My words sounded wooden.

Irie, although still a teenager, had a full beard and bright, active eyes. "We'll be seeing you, you know where." He turned, nodded at me, and left the classroom, his feet quickly and noisily trampling down the four flights of stairs, almost like a drum beat. Then silence, and finally we could even hear the bottom door open to Putnam Street and slam shut.

Who were "we?" And where was "where"?

"Do any of you guys know what he was talking about?" No one said anything, and then Sharon grabbed her hoodie and made the same exit, also nodding, giving the rest of the kids a sturdy stare, bordering on the same hostility that Irie had.

"Excuse me? Can someone tell me what is going on here?" No one did, and the students, I guess bonded in some way by country of origin, looked meaningfully at each other. Recognition. Just for a moment. They gathered their things too, dark colored book bags, light sweaters and purses, and they started leaving. "Hey! What are you doing? You can't just leave school." But they did, all but Ceejay. In my two years at Frederick Douglass, nothing like this had ever happened.

"Ceejay. Can you explain to me why everyone else just walked out of class?" I noticed my descent into heavy breathing and my voice sounding tight and high pitched. Ceejay looked amused.

"It isn't you, Mister. It has nothing to do with you. Trinidad and Jamaica. That's why they dipped. It's about heart and blood and revenge. You're a good teacher, Mister. But you're not more important. Less important."

Revenge for what? Then Ceejay walked a little closer to me. "Mister. I want to show you something." He moved the bottom of his long and open hoodie so I could see the brown butt of a gun. He turned the heat up, and at that, I began sweating even more.

"What?" My voice sounded unfamiliar. "What are you doing, Ceejay?"

"It's mine. Protection. You stay inside, Mister. You okay. But you can't fight this fight for us. You can't do anything."

What do teachers say when a student flashes a gun at them? What do they do? There must be a protocol or a correct response or even helpful words, but I didn't know any of them. Suddenly, I felt so unuseful, so completely naive and stupid. And scared, although I knew Ceejay didn't bring a gun to school for me.

"Ceejay. You could be arrested for bringing a gun into school. You know that, don't you?"

He smiled at me, and, taller, brought his hand down on my shoulder warmly, his pudgy smile showing all his teeth. I felt like a child. "Bless up," he said.

He left the way the other five kids did, and I sat down, but immediately stood up, then sat down, then got back up and walked over to the coffee maker, and realized it had been emptied. I knew schools had a procedure or teachers to leave in the middle of the school day, but I didn't know those either as I never had. I followed the kids down the stairwell and out the door, not to go find them, but to walk to the Jamaican cafe down the block. How can you be a teacher if you have no one to teach? Seven forty five now, I looked at my watch. I needed to get a cup, and return for my next class in 10 minutes, which has also had a low turnout. I didn't put on my jacket, just walked shirt-sleeves the one block to Frenchman's Cove, didn't make small talk with the owner, and walked back, shaky. Were the Tridadian kids going to fight the kids from Jamaica? Why would they do that? Would they shoot each other? Would they hurt each other? What would happen to Ceejay, to the sisters, to Irie? The trees on Marcy Avenue had a full complement of leaves, maples and ash, not really fall yet at all, the end of summer. Warm, but strangely, no cars driving up and down the street. Just warmth on my skin and a testy anxiety in my belly.

As I walked down Marcy to Putnam, I heard some yelling, and turned my head left, on Putnam toward Nostrand Avenue. I saw none of my kids. But I did see a crowd, a dozen boys, maybe, 15, kicking someone on the ground in the middle of the street there. There was a boy in that street, fallen and grunting. I saw one very tall boy–I guess I should call them young men, for they had the bodies of men–stand the other young man up from the ground and then punch him in the face, his arm reaching back and, in his white tee-shirt, land a blow with such force that I heard it like a pop. The sound sickened me, made me nauseous. I opened my mouth but nothing came out. The fighters started pummeling the stricken boy, body blows, and to his face. They wore shorts and sneakers, sunglasses, and flags over their faces. I didn't know the fist against a human could make such sounds. I expected a dampened thud but the fists sounded so much sharper than that, a sound that rang up the block to where I was standing, bouncing off the extra ornate and old red-brick high school building.

For the second time that day, I didn't know how to respond. I had the convenient thought that Ceejay spoke the truth, that this was not my fight. The boy went down again and the kicking started. Would he die? Would they kill him?

I ran. And felt worse for it. Down Marcy Ave into the official teacher entrance, by the school security officer, who was reading a New York Post, and then up the stairs, my heart beating with indecision and panicked confusion. When I got to the classroom, I locked the door, turned the CD player off and the lights out, although the overhead lights hardly made a difference with the morning in full bloom.

What a shielded person. What a stupid, inexperienced man. Of course teenagers fought each other. They always had, in high school all across the country, everywhere. That's what teenage boys did. "'Heart and blood and revenge,'" Ceejay had said. What did I know of it? It was not my fight, I kept repeating to myself.

I sat there in the empty classroom. No one in my second period class came in either. Eight o'clock. Eight fifteen. Eight thirty. Eight forty five.

I heard the plane crash into the first tower, which sounded like a bomb going off, or what I imagined a bomb sounded like, an explosion. But I felt too overwhelmed by the events right here in Brooklyn, so I did not look up.

HUINA ZHENG

RAINY DAY

It rained. For breakfast, we had *xiaolongbao*, and during snack time, we enjoyed cheese crackers. While waiting for the rain to stop, we sipped rich hot chocolate. Raindrops danced on the windows, creating a joyful spectacle. We captured our daughter, lost in lines and colors, drawing a birthday dinosaur. Her smile, the whisper of pens across paper, filled the room with life. We shared these pictures on our WeChat moments, the vibrant colors contrasting with the gray sky outside. We kissed her forehead, her soft skin carrying the milk-sweet scent. We snuggled on the couch, watching a tired mom and her stern mother-in-law argue on TV. Their expressions were overly dramatic, and their emotions too intense. You mentioned that you couldn't handle such melodramatic soap operas—reasons like excessive falseness and drama—and I told you that I had trimmed my hair last night, my bangs no longer covering my eyes, which surprised us both, the new finding that despite spending every day together, there were still many changes to notice. We turned off the TV and continued cuddling on the couch, discussing which restaurant to go to for dinner and which movie to watch tonight. However, the corner of the living room emitted occasional unpleasant odors from the hamster cage, assaulting our senses. I stood up and fetched a plastic bag from the kitchen. You suggested we change the hamster's bedding together. Holding our breath, we used a plastic spoon to transfer the soiled bedding from the cage into the bag, yellow stains visible on the white material. The curious hamster peered out from the cage, looking at us with its large, watery black eyes. We stroked its soft fur. You brewed a pot of oolong tea, and I played some music on my phone. I rested my head on your shoulder, feeling the warmth of your body. I narrated the love story of the main characters from the book I had been reading recently. Outside, rain performed a pitter-patter serenade on the leaves, a sound I anticipated would be irksome. Yet, as the performance persisted, its rhythm morphed into a comforting lullaby, its steady beats offering unexpected solace.

MAGGIE AND FRANK

The piercing siren of an ambulance awakens Maggie O'Shea from her nap; then the front door slams shut. She rises from the bed feeling unusually light on her feet and the pain in her chest is gone. "Lizzie?" she calls, but there's no answer. *Where could they have gone?*

In the living room she gazes at Frank's photo on the Day of the Dead altar while reclining in the old green wingback chair she's claimed in daughter Lizzie's home where she lives now that her husband Frank has died.

When Frank died it was as if her right arm had been amputated. The arm that fed her, the arm she wrote with, gardened with, played piano with. Like a person who has lost a limb still feels sensations in their phantom limb, she still feels Frank's presence and is shocked each time she realizes that no, he is not there. When she rolls over and reaches for his broad shoulders in bed, the empty space where he should be scares away her slumber. When she does sleep, she yearns to dream of him, but never does.

Her son-in-law, Vincente introduced her to the Mexican tradition of the Day of the Dead with their altar festooned with candles, Marigolds, Sugar skulls, and photographs of deceased family members. Maggie wanted to add the old wedding photo of her and Frank, but Vicente said it was bad luck to have the photo of a living person on the altar. Instead, they placed a snapshot of Frank from last year's Fourth of July picnic. That photo of him at the barbecue posing with a grin and holding up the spatula like a wand always makes her smile.

Next to the photos, small dishes with favorite foods of the deceased have been placed in anticipation of the return of their souls. The traditional belief is that this one night of the year the departed souls are allowed to return to the world of the living. A cheeseburger sits next to Franks picture.

Maggie aches for one more embrace, one more slow dance, one more time to lie with him in her big empty bed. In their sixty years together, they never slept apart. Tears flow through the deep lines of her face as she gazes at the snapshot of Frank grilling and grinning from ear to ear. Maggie lived all her adult life basking in the warmth of that smile. "Please visit me tonight, Frank, just this once."

He stands beside her chair. She rubs her eyes. Is he a ghost? He looks real, but is she asleep, dreaming? When he reaches for her hand and flashes that beautiful smile she doesn't care if it's a dream, she slips her hand in his and rises. With his arm tight against the small of her back he leads her across the living room floor in rhythm to the slow ballad playing on the smart speaker.

"I can't believe you're here," she whispers in his ear.

"I've been waiting for you, Sunshine."

"You, waiting for me?"

The front door opens, and Lizzie and Vince walk in, quietly. Maggie watches Lizzie move the wedding day photo from the bookshelf to the altar. Frank whispers, "A few more steps to the music, Sunshine, and off we'll go together." Maggie presses her hand once more into his.

OUR GRATEFUL DEAD STORY

Illustration by Skylar Kaster

Winner of the Summer 2024
Midsummer Dream House Fiction Contest

Five teenagers find adventure, friendship and something even more
extraordinary at a long-ago Grateful Dead concert.

1.

In the beginning there is terror.

That's right—none of the good stuff waiting just round the bend (adventure, fun, friendship), nor the many other shades of darkness that will also visit along the way. Only terror.

There in the last row of the deepest corner of the furthest parking lot—if you look just right you can see it rising in waves, up along the sides of a parked Winnebago. Underneath which our four young men are presently convened; bodies sprawled and tangled, cheeks pressed against fractured pavement.

This for what feels like a thousand years (but is in fact minutes, about twenty-five). Until Len ventures out, comes back mumbling that those they're hiding from are nowhere in sight.

So then Shlag is up and out too, shaking off mud as he talks about a way the evening can be salvaged. A simple plan, apparently, is all that's needed. Something he, Shlag, just happens to have: nearby bar famous for not checking ID's. Nachos that probably will not be disappointing. Hofstra girls, supposedly quite cool, and, like, extremely open-minded.

Len pays rapt attention, says, "So the concert—you don't want to go?"

These words for Shlag a kind of punch—making him flinch, wobble, then hold out his fingernails and thereupon scan as if he were alone, without care, on the moon. And though this is partially explained by the mere fact that Len has taken him seriously, far more is the question itself, and a related proposition that to Shlag's mind should not really be open for debate: this concert, and their attempt to be a part, is a total fucking fiasco. Evident too soon after they'd popped out of Sambursky's mom's van, slipped through the gate, hit the parking lot scene.

The parking lot scene. An ice cream sundae of a good time comprised of one scoop block party, one scoop open-air bazaar, one scoop Woodstock re-creation that together, all reports had indicated, just might be greater, madder, more momentous then the concert itself.

Yet was Shlag the only one? Pretending from the get-go that this is what was gotten? And so ignoring that between expectation and reality there had been certain holes? Holes so large and obvious as to be weirdly hard to notice?

Berger accused of stealing a bumper sticker, then tripping over an old dog as he backed away. Len mistaken for a narc—a narc!—then cursed and spat on even as it became clear that he was not a narc but instead a mountain-sized teenager wearing the wrong clothes, okay, sure, you got us, a sus-piciously new tie-dye shirt, jeans, army jacket, all of which, no doubt, his mom, Mrs. Borax, had starched and ironed to near weapon-grade density… But a narc?

Then, turning a corner, and encountering a pack of guys lead by Chuck Piccolini—with this arguably deserving its own litany, a litany of far more serious shit because Chuck Piccolini is a psychopath and quite possibly a murderer who has beaten up half of Nassau county, including two guys he left with brain dam-age—and Chuck hates Sambursky. Why? Good question, and regarding which Sambursky himself is quite curious. Yet, despite multiple inquiries made through several back channels, no answer is forthcoming. Only a sentence. Sambursky gets a beating.

Len looks to Berger, who is also now out from hiding.

Berger at ease but also, Len can tell, ready to take some action, do something, anything. This analysis, however, largely horrendous. As in truth, while the two stand nodding, bobbing, ceremoniously spitting, Berger is com-piling a 'best of' from the silent self-excoriation that's been ongoing since this whole Piccolini thing began. And while Berger's compilation, his 'best of' is rich in variety, there is to it but a single theme: that there are no limits, nor will there ever be, to the bad things his life can, will, must be.

Len squeezes Berger's shoulder, walks up again to the Winnebago's front bumper, looks out, sighs—as nothing he now sees strikes him as anything but okay, promising. The carpet of parked cars stretching out pretty much for-ever. Silver-blue twilight, with alluring stuff—Frisbees, balloons, kites—moving through it. And people too, mostly in groups, near but not too near, and all of whom upon closer scrutiny are grinning, cutting up, laughing, experiencing, there's nothing else to call it, some kind of fun.

So now it's with a measure of urgency that Len brings Berger together with Shlag and bids the latter to again share his vision to salvage the evening. With Shlag abiding. Indeed, doing so in a burst of spirit that makes his entire body tremble. And imbues too, it seems, the vision itself, as it now boasts a handful of undeniable upgrades: crazy-cheap kamikaze shots, near-definite New York Islanders and New York Jets player sightings, Space Invaders…

After, Len raises an eyebrow, "Pretty good, yeah?"

"Yeah," says Berger, "but—"

"But?" says Shlag.

"I'm going home."

"Come again," says Len.

"Home. Me," says Berger.

"Impossible," says Shlag. "How the hell you gonna get there?"

Berger shrugs.

"You don't know?" says Shlag. "You don't know?!"

Berger nods.

"Right, okay," says Shlag, suddenly pensive. "Hey, on second thought, I'm coming with you."

"Whoa, hold on," says Len. "I admit this is totally fucked, yet..."

"Yet?" repeats Shlag.

"Yeah," says Berger, "yet what?"

All three then go quiet, and remain so much longer than typical, which in turn creates an environment that is pretty much ideal for something each tends to do anyway: let fly their imaginations. So conjure, for example, that the location they presently find themselves—a parking lot, wedged between an old Winnebago and rusted van—is also, at the same time, somewhere, something far different. The inner chamber, for instance, of a fantastical seashell—with an equally fantastical ambient roar, comprised of faraway voices, drumming, boom boxes, car stereos.

And what each further discovers is really how compelling such an environment can be. And so also how easy it is to do what each now does: go further. And so for forty, fifty seconds, avoiding eye contact and feigning nonchalance, stand and shuffle about. With this now amplifying each's ability to perceive this or that smell or sound or trick of light, and also the way the feel and flow of these perceptions serves as a kind of crazy-beautiful soundtrack to the bits and pieces of thought floating in their heads...

All until from behind the Winnebago's rear bumper Sambursky appears, ambles over, says, "So?"

"So what?"

"How come you dingle-berries don't ask what I want to do?"

"Okay," says Len.

"The concert," says Sambursky. "Let's go."

"You're joking," says Berger.

Sambursky lets this hang—then grimaces, blinks, takes out his purple porcelain pipe and, with fingers only slightly atremble, packs it with a pinch of pot; this before slowly, carefully, one by one, flicking out the seeds. All a means for Sambursky to buy a few more seconds: make one last wiggle against a grip he has now for weeks felt closing. This grip being a gambler's grip, whose prevailing aspects—faith, illogic, intimations of cosmic glory—feel to Sambursky far too familiar, far too warm and cozy, for him to really want out of.

2.

Inside, the thought is mostly of escape.

Instantly, even while passing through the turnstile into the atom-smasher chaos of the arena's outer ring, where the name of the game is dodging bodies barreling from all directions while also shooting the traffic's flashing gaps. Yet where to? This the conundrum, as presently they find their attention occupied by a whole host of concerns. Examples: not encountering Chuck Piccolini; not losing their ticket stubs; not walking into anything or anybody; appearing more or less unbothered by the various shouts aimed at or near their faces.

Then, through a tunnel, something totally unexpected: a headlong encounter with a notable, even quite marvelous architectural work (something not all that common on Long Island): the massive vaulting chamber of a fifteen thousand seat arena. Tendering that in which their day-to-day lives are perhaps just a bit deficient—a most extraordinary scale. Of steel! Concrete! Civic pride! Engineering and construction chops! Not to mention enclosed open space—cubed acre after cubed acre. With all this coalescing with the Human—as the audience is more than half assembled—to create a wholly distinct ambiance. Ambiance, as compared to the arena's outer ring, that could hardly be more different. Ambiance permeated by an overt sense of expansiveness, anticipation, muted glee, temporary community; and also, not least, a kind of high-frequency, mid-voltage, mad, happy, nutty, semi-peaceful thrum.

Regarding any of this, however, the four's reaction is blah...

And as they trudge on each grows the distance between himself and the group. This until they reach their aisle, take seats, slink down as low as the laws of physics permit and scan the arena for Chuck Piccolini.

Then, not finding him, scan again, over and over, with this soon causing them to spot people they do recognize. Many, from school and town. And most of whom they're not displeased to see. As most, in terms of currency, social currency, are in some way interesting. Further, this activity itself—the mere perusal of the audience without finding Chuck Piccolini—quickly reveals itself to be its own kind of fun. Then becomes a sport, the rules of which all somehow intuitively understand: Number one, spot someone you recognize. Number two, speak their name in a manner indicating you mostly don't care. Hey there's Wolf. Fox. Nan Silver. Nick Something. Vogelfry. Cindy Hurwitz. Zipper. Stone. Vic Rizzo. New Girl From Texas. Skinny Vinny. Adam Funk. Aardvark.

And they joke about Paul—goaded by the empty seat in their midst and also, in school, the Hollywood pose Paul struck while informing he'd make his own way to the arena. Yet also because Paul's participation is not even their idea. That whereas the four of them can at least claim to have come together semi-normally—feeling each other out over months—Paul has been imposed from above. By McFarland, their English teacher, who in his inimitable half-hippie half-Nazi way made it clear that there would be consequences if an invitation were not extended to the new kid in town.

The jokes fly scattershot, though also, as if guided by some Junior High versions of themselves they can't yet quite control, come to land on a single theme: the obscure, intricate, anatomically impossible, entirely imaginary sex acts in which Paul and McFarland are at this very instant engaged. And for this a group mind emerges, as each loses himself in a fury of riffing at once mean-spirited, creative, unconsciously arousing. With this phenomenon then fitfully ex hausting itself, before halting altogether not four seconds before Paul appears, grinning, at the foot of the aisle.

Len and Berger stand, make inquiry as to where he's been.

"All about."

"Doing?" says Len.

"And your eyes," says Berger, "what's up there?"

"Whose question first?" says Paul.

Len and Berger shrug.

"Talking, walking, thinking—yeah, definitely," says Paul. "...I've been just, you know, kicking my own tires..."

Paul then emits a sound—a sort of slow-building, richly baritone snicker; and while he gently rocks Len and Berger catch eyes, query one another—what the hell?

Then, an instant later, as Paul steps into the aisle, Len raises an arm. "Your eyes... what is up?"

"Psilocybin is what I think you're referring to," says Paul.

Len grimaces.

"The psychoactive element in mushrooms," says Paul.

"So then, you're on magic acid-mushrooms," says Berger.

"What you just said," says Paul, "are two different things."

"Of course. But you're on one of them?"

"I am."

"What's it like?"

"Can't say yet."

Len and Berger, ever slightly, pout.

"No, look, hey," says Paul. "What I mean is, maybe really, they haven't kicked in yet."

"Why?"

"Well, for one thing, I might've botched the dose."

"Dose?"

"Yeah."

"Botched it?"

"Indeed."

3.

Then, at once, the lights above extinguish and those of the assembled thousands not already standing and facing the stage do so, many raising lit matches or lighters as the musicians amble into view and with just a slight acknowledgment of the audience ready themselves and begin to play a song that cannot be well heard. That sounds, is, tinny, distant, hollow. Yet, shortly, as if some unseen switch has been flicked or socket plugged, bounds out fully, with an overwhelming amplitude, in a bouncy bluesy melody surprisingly mid-tempo for the opening song of a rock concert.

And Len, Shlag, Berger, Sambursky and Paul are with it—clapping, stomping, howling.

More even, each ventures an act that is among the most meaningful of his life. In that it represents a clean break with his past. Renders him a stone liar vis-a-vis something he has claimed he'd never do. And also, no less, will prompt a reassessment, and then the taking of the exact opposite position on one of the most divisive social issues of the day. Dancing. Right now, each is dancing.

Yet also, at the very same time—not one of them is truly with it.

That none is really dressed correctly, or knows the music, or is dancing naturally, or, by all appearances, even an iota as transported as everyone else in sight—these facts can't help but get a little in the way. Then a lot in the way. Then, as facts sometimes can, animate and take to the air—dashing and darting before coming in close to whisper the same in each of their ears: Hey! You! Dipshit. This thing, their thing, cannot be your thing. It's too nuanced. Too inside. Besides, are you joking? The Grateful Dead? In 1979?! The time to have climbed on the bus has long since passed by…

Still though, it's easy enough to fake it. Which is what they do: nodding, grinning, bobbing, dancing very badly.

Each that is with the exception of Shlag.

Shlag, who now stands bug-eyed, catatonic. Staring into an oncoming apocalypse…

Parents! His, Ty and Dot, whom he hates and loves and hates—tonight are going to lower the boom. Fact. So much do they detest who and what they perceive him to be (drug user, drug-music lover, fading honor roll student), his current interests (drugs, drug-music, unfathomable depravities) and where it's all most certainly heading (Creedmoor, Sing Sing, Mount Zion Cemetery) that tonight, without doubt, these two, fucking Ty and fucking Dot, will start to do things: call these guys' parents; destroy his records (philistines!); make good even—I think they could—on the military school thing…

"Hey, Shlag, talk to me," says Len, kindly, but also while staring at the stage. This though hardly mattering as already Shlag is lowering himself to the floor where, reaching it, he slaps his own face, then cups his hands over his eyes.

Yet now here is Paul, kneeling.

Paul, not with any particular plan, but indeed something of the opposite. Or, as he was just thinking of it, 'a plans suck worldview'. But, perhaps that's enough. As now it's with sure hands, delicacy, even grace that Paul reaches out and guides Shlag's cupped hands up and away from his eyes.

Shlag letting him, mostly because it's something he's about to do anyway, but also something else, having to do with this other kid, that about him, this Paul, beyond the nutty-bizzaro stuff—there's something maybe okay.

After, Paul sits next to Shlag, begins to sway. Shlag just watching, not knowing how to act but not needing to as Paul tilts forward, whispers, "Hey man."

Paul then leaning in, close, closer, closer still, smiling, stating with perfect matter-of-factness: "It's too late."

Fuck you! This Shlag's first three thoughts, followed by I don't know what you mean! Indeed, the last he actually begins to say, yet stops before finishing, because, well…

Shlag now stares deeply into his work boots, paws a patch of ink-stained leather, then lets himself tip forward so that his forehead hovers just above his ankles. Shlag remaining this way for many seconds until, on a sudden bolt, he whips back his torso and head and shouts up into the arena's steel black firmament the same three words Paul said to him, only now in the form of a question.

"Yeah. Yeah." Paul raves back.

"But!"

"What?!"

"Since when?

Paul shrugs.

"You don't know?" says Shlag.

Paul bobs.

Shlag now suddenly outraged. "Come on, really, tell me the truth."

Paul gives no reply.

"How can that be?! How can you not know…"

Paul smiles.

Shlag bewildered, but not for very long, as he also begins to smile.

The two then scooching this way and that, getting comfy on the floor, all so afterward they can more enjoyably lounge, banter, close their eyes, concentrate on the music, think inane, profound, inane thoughts. On and on they go, for minutes, lifetimes, minutes, until suddenly, with nary a nod of coordination, Shlag and Paul rise in perfect time and look out over the heads of the boys and girls dancing in front of them.

And what they encounter, everything, seems totally different.

And later, when this moment is analyzed, often Paul and Shlag will quibble over this or that detail; yet always, regarding what is most significant, they will only ever agree. Which is that suddenly, in this thumping, swinging, hurtling moment, to an extent neither had been previously able, both Paul and Shlag can see. So that here is the band, these almost-old sort-of-fragile six guys, the Grateful Dead—far away but also perfectly clear, playing some slow-going hooked-out happy-loser's lament and appearing, if still not like normal rock performers, then at least as if they're finally fully awake, totally engaged, and perhaps having a slightly better than average evening.

And the audience, here too is difference. As while the majority are still focused upon the band and every gesture they make, a goodly portion is not. Instead is roaming about the arena, congregating in tunnels, drinking, smoking, fooling around. Dancing still, of course, but also, as far as what they're dancing to is concerned, treating its source as if it were some unseen, supersonic, providentially-supplied stereo system. So that now if a person were to slowly scan about this venue what they'd see would resemble nothing so much as a party, an enormous party over which absolutely no one—least of all the Grateful Dead—is in charge.

So Paul and Shlag jump in.

And in doing so find that Len, Berger, Sambursky are already there—dancing and stomping about as if their aisle were some inflatable kiddie pool. Yowling, scowling, smiling, and also, by way of movement, posture, glint of eye, making truest heart declarations as to that of which Chaos it is—but that of a stripe neither has ever before encountered: loose, spirited, uthey're presently afraid (nada), the earthly forces that could possibly stop them from doing what they're right now doing (ibid), when exactly it is they'd expect this current state of being and also the sense of life and possibility it engenders to come to an end (hint: no time soon).

4.

Yet then the lights are up, and after a stilted ninety seconds, during which no one speaks nor looks at one another, the five file out of the row and begin to walk around. Walking with great urgency and purpose (although, of course, they have neither). And walking too with increasing speed, until, as they near completion of an entire revolution of the Coliseum's outer ring, they come upon a gap in the interior wall. A cul-de-sac tightly packed with people they kind of, sort of, know.

Len, Sambursky, Paul rush right in, and so are vanished instantly by the churning crowd.

While Berger and Shlag abruptly break stride, halt, then fidget at the threshold, not quite believing what they see.

Chaos it is—but that of a stripe neither has ever before encountered: loose, spirited, unself-aware. Also, and no small detail: chaos wherein all social bounds have been as if magically filleted. How else to explain the present sight of Len, Sambursky and Paul? Their talking, smiling, laughing with person after person whom they most certainly don't typically talk, smile, laugh. Kaleidoscopically then, in and out of Berger and Shlag's narrow lines of vision, amped-up human after amped-up human pops in and out of view: Warren Wolf / Adam Funk / Nick Vogelfry / Zipperman / Fox / Nan Silver / Wendy Cohen / Martino / New Girl From Texas / Kozak / Debbie Horsley / Aardvark...

Oh, all this a reach away from someone leaning against a large tray rack, laughing, holding hands, making out with an old person (no joke, a woman who could easily be thirty years old), with this someone happening to be Chuck Piccolini.

The same.

Though perhaps not—as it's this particular sight that proves to be just a bit too much. Suggesting the very real possibility that at present, what's actually happening, is some kind of collective hallucination.

Can they too play along? Berger and Shlag catch eyes, shrug, grimace, sway. Yet, before any further deliberation can take place, all is rendered moot, as two people pop out of the crush, approach, say in near perfect harmony, "Don't we know you?"

"Know us?" says Berger.

Cindy Hurwitz nods.

"Well, depends," says Shlag, "what you mean by 'know'. If you mean, have we been in the same schools, classes, buses, cafeterias and pretty much seen each other every day for the last eleven years—then yeah, sure, you know us."

Nan Silver barely blinks, deadpans, "Of course, but not 'know know'".

Shlag falls in love, instantly and also for the rest of his life, and so launches three new riffs, simultaneously, all on topics not particularly clear. And while Nan Silver indulges, Cindy Hurwitz does not, instead whips her back at Shlag, looks at Berger, says, "Okay, definitely, your hair."

Berger murmurs.

"The length—it's... good. Majorly."

"My hair?"

"Yes."

"Its length?"

"Yup."

"Majorly?"

"Correct."

Berger looks about, interested if anyone can overhear.

"Very Bobby Weir," says Cindy. "That's how it looks."

"…thanks."

"And of course I remember you. From math."

"Yeah?"

"You were one of the smart ones."

"Bad thing?" says Berger.

"No, of course not," says Cindy. "Well… maybe."

Each holds down a grin as Cindy asks what number show this is for him.

"First. You?"

"Sixth."

"Wow. That's a lot."

"Not really," says Cindy, "I know a guy whose seen four hundred and eighty-six."

"Okay, right—that's a lot."

"But wait—number one? You have to tell me, how was your first set?"

Berger now almost pleased—the way the conversation is maybe going, that he's not yet stepped on this girl's toes or forgotten to swallow. But then, more, by a thrill taking hold, knowing that he's about to do something that before tonight was likely unthinkable—that is, reveal to Cindy, reveal to anyone, something of his soul.

"Want to know?" says Berger.

"I do," says Cindy. "Definitely."

Berger takes a breath, opens his mouth, yet before even the first syllable takes shape can't but acknowledge the moment has passed. As somehow, the exact spot he and Cindy occupy has become some kind of unofficial rallying point. So that all around them are bodies—overpowering the air with scents of cigarettes, shampoo, sweat, essential oils, cologne, Bazooka bubble gum, youth. Bodies threshing and pressing and thereby creating a shared kinetic charge all the more potent because most of these people, by far the majority, still don't really know each other. First comes Wolf and Fox and Wendy Cohen and Debbie Kirkovsky and Funk. Then: Nan Silver, Shlag, Paul, Len, Vogelfry. Then Zipperman, Rizzo, Kozak, Skinny Vinny, New Girl From Texas, Aardvark.

Surrender—this would seem Berger and Cindy's only option. And hereafter, along with everyone else, they bumble about this randomly chosen patch of concrete floor. Until an instant arrives when as if by wolf pack telepathy this same assemblage steps back and re-configures into the shape of a near-perfect paisley, and thereafter remain glancing at one another at first with semi-concealed mirth and self-satisfaction but then, as seconds pass, a squirreliness and mounting unease. This until Fox looks toward Len and makes serious inquiry as to how later he plans on getting home.

"Shlag's dad—why? Need a ride?" this from Sambursky, as he jogs into the paisley's center.

Fox grunts.

"Cool, cause Shlag's dad would love to give you one, right Shlag?"

Shlag goes still.

"See? That settles it. Just meet us at the flag poles after the concert."

"How many can he fit?" says Kozak.

Sambursky ponders. "Twenty, thirty, it's a clown car, so we'll make it work."

There's laughter, thank you's.

"No problem," says Sambursky, hugging Shlag from behind, saying: "People! As we pile into the car there has to be like a totally concerted effort not to say the wrong thing. Got it? No like 'Hey Mr. Hammershlag, do you mind if we get stoned?' No 'Yo, Mr. H., crank up the tunes.' No, 'Hey old fucking geezer, turn on some Grateful Dead!'"

5.

Is there more? Uh huh. Beyond what can be imagined or remembered.

Starting with the second set: how back at the seats, Paul, Shlag, Berger, Sambursky and Len are greeted with a suspicious degree of sincerity by some old hippie-types seated nearby (several of whom, over the decades, will become good friends). And also, not long after the band ambles back on stage and begins to play again, all five find themselves psychically undone by an extended interlude of extreme sonic weirdness. An assault, no, an ordeal, that feels like it will never end; but then, of course, does. Facilitated by the band and their deft transformation of the sonic weirdness into actual songs—a cathartic run of the soulful and/or danceable variety.

Then, afterward, outside the arena, as they approach the flag poles, Sambursky out front, howling, halting every so often to glad-hand passing strangers…

It's a stealth attack and, in the context of Chuck Piccolini's larger body of work, somewhat modest in scope. That is, it's comprised of a single blow, and once delivered, instead of engaging in some kind of humiliation ritual (a common flourish), Chuck just turns and skips away.

Nonetheless, in the aftermath, Sambursky is on his ass, gazing up into a humongous crowd, with that which had recently been his nose resembling nothing so much as a hunk of raw chicken breast, with a narrow slit, gurgling blood. An injury that will not only curtail the rest of Sambursky's evening but also cost him the rest of his life—in pain, appearance, surgeries. And yet, also an injury about which over the years Sambursky never complained. To the contrary, it was almost as if Sambursky came to feel his wound as largely something good. Good in the way it sealed his connection to the band, conferred upon it a kind of validity, even purity.

Also—the rendezvous is made, the one planned at intermission. Yet somehow now the number of kids has more than quadrupled and the prevailing spirit, that too has morphed. Example: presently the notion of getting into some parent's car has to it a whiff of unspeakable heresy. As in this new epoch, this new way of being, now only seconds old, the one true option would seem to be that they walk home.

Which is what happens: a five hour trek, mostly along a highway, made by an initially large, unruly, ecstatic but steadily diminishing tribe. Including among Cindy Hurwitz and Berger, who share conversation and also for most of the five hours bump thighs, hands, shoulders until finally, at Cindy's corner, they stop, face off, swallow carefully and inhabiting the very outer bounds of how close people can come to kissing without doing so, say, "see ya Monday".

But these are mere facts.

And what this story cares most about dwells elsewhere, in a truth that on this evening, in the strange, inane, profound, violent, beautiful, funny, ultimately undefinable universe of the Grateful Dead, certain people appeared and came together. People now forever connected.

And this, our story, is part of something even larger. Something that is open, and alive, that has not, nor will ever be, captured.

And so, continues.

BIOGRAPHIES

JEFFREY ZABLE is a teacher, conga drummer/percussionist who plays for dance classes and rumbas around the San Francisco Bay Area, and a writer of poetry, flash-fiction, and non-fiction. He's published five chapbooks and his writing has appeared in hundreds of literary magazines and anthologies, more recently in *Chewers & Masticadores, Linked Verse, Ranger, Cacti Fur, Uppagus,* and many others.

SHAUN ANTHONY MCMICHAEL has taught writing to students since 2007 from around the world, in classrooms, juvenile detention halls, mental health treatment centers, and homeless youth drop-ins throughout the Seattle area. Over 90 of his poems, short stories, and reviews have appeared in literary magazines, online, and in print, including the forthcoming short story collection *The Wild Familiar* (Fall, 2024; CJ Press). He lives in Seattle with his wife and son.

SUT PHAL is a self-published author on Amazon Kindle Direct Publishing. Some of his individual artworks have also been published in *PoetSpeak Magazine* and *Leafy Leaf Magazine.* He is also a spoken word artist with a passion for performance, poetry, storytelling, lyrics, music, and content creation on YouTube.

STARRY KRUEGER is a San Diego based writer, teacher and director. She is the founder of Imaginary Theater Company, a theater company committed to producing original plays that empower children to be the heroes of their own stories. Her plays *Dream Train, Mama Threw Me So High, He Who Speaks* and *Canary Cockroach Phoenix* have been published by Drama Notebook. *Dream Train* recently celebrated its first international production in Morocco. Starry is a proud member of the Dramatist's Guild and TYA/USA. Instagram: @imaginarytheaterco

PAUL HOSTOVSKY's poems have won a Pushcart Prize, two Best of the Net Awards, the FutureCycle Poetry Book Prize, and have been featured on *Poetry Daily, Verse Daily, The Writer's Almanac,* and the *Best American Poetry* blog. He makes his living in Boston as a sign language interpreter.

NICHOLAS GROOMS is a poet, writer and musician hailing from Garden City, Kansas. He has appeared in such periodicals as *Verse Libre Quarterly, Skyline Magazine, On Gossamer Wings* and the *Southwest Review* (KS), though he is most well known for his work as a musician, creating music for the Kansas City Chiefs. Grooms currently resides in Austin, TX with his wife Sarah and their two children, forever learning and growing in his favorite role of "proud father."

JOHN GREY is an Australian poet, US resident, recently published in *New World Writing, North Dakota Quarterly* and *Lost Pilots.* Latest books, *Between Two Fires, Covert* and *Memory Outside The Head* are available through Amazon. Work upcoming in *California Quarterly, Seventh Quarry, La Presa* and *Doubly Mad.*

BRANDON INGALLS is an emergency medicine physician living in Chicago.

JC REILLY's most recent collection is *Amo e Canto,* winner of the Sow's Ear Poetry prize. She has work published or forthcoming from *CAROUSEL, Dunes Review, Great River Review,* and elsewhere. Follow her on Twitter @Aishatonu and on Bluesky @Aishatonu.bsky.social. Or follow her cats on IG @jc.reilly

MARCOS ORO is an emerging, New Jersey poet, and artist. Presently he is working on a collection of poems. It would be his first book. You may see one, of several, of his, art collections on LinkedIn.

JERRY CHIEMEKE is a Nigerian writer, communications specialist, film critic, journalist and lawyer. His work has appeared in *Die Welt, The i Paper, Icefloe Press, Kissing Dynamite Poetry, Inlandia Journal, The Maryland Review, Serotonin Poetry, Brittlepaper* and elsewhere. Jerry is the author of the short story collection *Dreaming of Ways to Understand You* and the poetry chapbook *Notes for Nnedimma.* He lives in London. Twitter: @J_Chiemeke Instagram: @j_chiemeke

JONATHAN WOO is a human being ('in case you were wondering' - from Jonathan). He has recently decided to pick up the pen after many years of only being a reader. He's interested in revealing stories that hide themselves in the ephemeral. His obsessions include Towers, photographs taken at dusk and the loch ness monster.

BIOGRAPHIES

GARTH WOLKOFF is a writer living in Brooklyn. He has a daughter, a job, and a coffee pot. He has published work in the *Indiana Review, Downtown Brooklyn Mr. Bull,* and *86 Logic.* He was a finalist for the Fractured Lit Winter Fast Flash Challenge, second place in the 2023 Fiction Potluck on the Writer's Workout website, and has a story coming out in *Every Day Fiction.*

HUINA ZHENG, a Distinction M.A. in English Studies holder, works as a college essay coach. She's also an editor at *Bewildering Stories.* Her stories have been published in *Baltimore Review, Variant Literature, Midway Journal,* and others. Her work has received nominations twice for both the Pushcart Prize and Best of the Net. She resides in Guangzhou, China with her husband and daughter.

CRYSTAL W. PILLIFANT has a master's degree in elementary education and taught for nearly twenty years in a bilingual school in the Beaverton School District near Portland, Oregon. After retiring, she wrote an autobiographical novel, *Maestra*, inspired by her experiences in the bilingual classroom. Other published works of hers have appeared in the *Persimmon Tree* online magazine. She lives in Port Townsend, Washington on the Puget Sound with her husband, Leo and two cats.

KEVIN MANDEL writes fiction and essays. His writing has appeared in *Playboy Magazine, New York Press, Joyland Magazine, Oldster Magazine, Vol. 1 Brooklyn and The Millions*; been featured in *Longreads* and *The Rumpus'* This Week in Short Fiction; placed as a semi-finalist for American Short Fiction's Halifax Ranch Fiction Prize.

EDWARD MICHAEL SUPRANOWICZ is the grandson of Irish and Lithuanian/Russian/Ukrainian immigrants. He grew up on a small farm in Appalachia. He has a grad background in painting and printmaking. Some of his artwork has recently or will soon appear in *Fish Food, Streetlight, Another Chicago Magazine, Door Is A Jar, The Phoenix,* and *The Harvard Advocate.* Edward is also a published poet who has had over 700 poems published and been nominated for the Pushcart Prize multiple times.

ASHLEY KAPLAN is a San Diego based photographer who specializes in working to empower the subjects she works with. She has been working as a photographer for eight years, and full time for two years. Ashley enjoys all things photography and the majority of the time you will find her with a camera in hand. If you catch her on the occasional moment without a camera in tow, you might find her running, hiking, painting, and hanging out with friends. To find more of Ashley's work, please find her on Instagram @kaplan.photographyy

PIA QUINTANO is a NYC-based writer/painter who is especially interested in humorous narratives in her visual work. Her paintings were sold at the Frank J.Miele Contemporary American Folk Art Gallery in NYC until it closed.

.